The Jungle Book

By Rudyard Kipling

Retold by G. C. Barrett

Illustrated by Don Daily

COURAGE
BOOKS

AN IMPRINT OF RUNNING PRESS
PHILADELPHIA · LONDON

To Anita and Quintin for their love and support
and to my daughter Susie—my Mowgli
—Don Daily

Contents

Introduction

Once you've read this story, you'll never think about a jungle in the same way again. The forests of India, where *The Jungle Book* takes place, were one of Rudyard Kipling's favorite places. He was born in India, and lived there until he was eight years old. He and his family then returned to their native country, England, but Rudyard never forgot India. He later returned there for seven more years, exploring and writing stories and poems.

Rudyard's time in India taught him to look at the world in new and imaginative ways. When he wrote *The Jungle Book*, he transformed the forest into a place where the animals have their own society. Into this fantastic world comes Mowgli, a human boy. Growing up among the animals, Mowgli has adventures that no human has ever known. Even though he becomes more and more aware that his animal friends are very different from himself, Mowgli learns to seek out the best that they have to offer, and return it with affection.

The Jungle Book is a story of discovery. It tells of learning new things about the place you know best. It's about exploring friendships, and using your imagination. So as you open these pages, open your mind to the possibilities all around you.

—G. C. Barrett

Mowgli's Brothers

One warm evening, high in the hills of India, Father Wolf woke from his day's rest and yawned. Mother Wolf lay with her gray nose dropped over her four tumbling cubs. Suddenly, down the hill, they heard the snarl of a tiger.

"What is Shere Khan doing here? He has no right!" Father Wolf said angrily. Shere Khan was the tiger who lived up the Waingunga River. "By the Law of the Jungle, he must give warning. He will frighten away the game."

"Shere Khan hunts cattle," said Mother Wolf. "The villagers from up the river will be very angry with him."

Down the hill, they could hear Shere Khan make a low, humming purr.

"H'sh," said Mother Wolf. She knew what the strange purr meant. "Shere Khan does not hunt cattle tonight. He hunts humans!"

This was serious, for The Law of the Jungle forbids every beast to hunt humans. Human-hunting means that, sooner or later, more humans will come, with guns and torches. Then everyone in the Jungle suffers.

"Something is coming," said Mother Wolf. "Get ready."

The bushes rustled, and Father Wolf sprang. But he had not seen what he was jumping at, and tried to stop in mid-leap. He landed on his rump.

"A human's cub!" he snapped. "Look!"

Directly in front of him stood a baby who could barely walk. He had black hair, and mischievous eyes. He looked up into Father Wolf's face and laughed.

"I have never seen one," said Mother Wolf. "Bring it here."

Father Wolf nudged the child into the cave, among the wolf cubs. The boy began playing with them, looking quite at home.

Then the moonlight was blocked out of the mouth of the cave. Shere Khan thrust his great head and shoulders into the small entrance.

"The man-cub's parents have run off," snarled Shere Khan. "Give it to me!"

"Wolves take orders only from the Head of the Pack," said Father Wolf. "The human's cub is ours."

"No!" The tiger's angry roar filled the cave with thunder. Mother Wolf sprang forward. Her eyes shone like two green moons in the darkness.

"The man's cub is mine!" she growled. "He will run with the Pack. And in the end, you frog-eater, he will hunt *you!*"

Shere Khan snarled. "We will see what the Pack has to say about this. The cub is mine, you bush-tailed thieves!" And he was gone.

Father Wolf stared at the child. "Should we keep him?" he asked.

"Keep him!" Mother Wolf gasped. "He came here alone, yet he was not afraid. I will keep him.

"Lie still, little frog," she said to the child, who had curled up next to her. "Yes, I will call you Mowgli the Frog."

"I wonder what the Pack will say," mused Father Wolf.

The Law of the Jungle says that every young cub must be introduced at the Pack Council, held each month on the night of the full moon. So Father and Mother Wolf waited until their cubs could run a little, and on the proper night they took Mowgli and his brothers to the Council Rock.

The Council Rock was a hilltop covered with boulders and stones. Akela, the great gray Lone Wolf, lay out at full length on the rock. He led the Pack with strength and wisdom. Below him were more than forty adult wolves, sitting and lounging in a circle.

"Look well, O Wolves!" cried Akela. At this urging, the parents nudged their cubs forward. The cubs tumbled and played in the moonlight as the senior wolves approved. Finally Father Wolf could wait no longer. Gently he pushed Mowgli into the center, where the boy began playing with some pebbles.

Akela never raised his head from his paws. All he said was: "Look well!"

But a muffled roar came up behind him. From the shadows, Shere Khan cried, "The cub is mine! Why does the Pack want a human's cub?"

Akela did not even twitch his ears. He said: "Wolves! Only the Pack decides what the Pack will do. The Law says that if there is a dispute about a cub, it must be spoken for by two members of the Pack. Who speaks for this cub?"

At the edge of the circle, a sleepy brown bear rose up on his hind quarters. This was Baloo. He was allowed in the Council because he taught the Law of the Jungle to the cubs.

"*I* speak for the man-cub. There is no harm in him. I will teach him myself."

"Who else speaks?" said Akela.

A shadow dropped down into the circle. It was Bagheera the Black Panther. Everyone knew him, and no one cared to cross his path, for Bagheera was cunning, and bold, and reckless. But he had a voice as soft as wild honey dripping from a tree, and fur softer than down.

"Akela," he purred, "the Law says if there is a dispute about a new cub, it may be settled with a gift. To Baloo's word I will add a newly killed bull. Will you accept the cub?"

There was a babble of voices. One by one the wolves sniffed Mowgli approvingly, and then went down the hill to share Bagheera's bull. Finally only Akela, Bagheera, Baloo, and Mowgli's new parents were left. With a roar of anger, Shere Khan quickly slunk away.

"This cub may help us one day in a time of need," said Akela. "Go, and teach him well."

And this was how Mowgli entered the Wolf-pack—with the love of adopted parents, a gift, and Baloo's good word.

Kaa's Hunting

Mowgli lived a wonderful life among the wolves. When he was not playing, he sat out in the sun and slept, and then ate and slept again. When he felt dirty or hot, he swam in the forest pools.

Baloo was delighted to have Mowgli as a pupil, for Mowgli was a quick learner. Baloo taught young Mowgli all kinds of things, like the hunting-calls, and how to climb, and how to get honey without being stung.

"I am teaching Mowgli the Master Words," Baloo told Bagheera one day. "He can now ask for help from all the Jungle-People, if he remembers the words."

"I am more likely to give help than to ask for it," said Bagheera, admiring his sharp talons. "Still I should like to hear them."

Baloo called to Mowgli, who was sulking under a tree. Baloo had to be stern when he taught, for the Law of the Jungle is serious business. That day, Mowgli had grown tired of his teacher's proddings.

"I come for Bagheera, not for you, fat old Baloo!" grumbled Mowgli.

"I do not care," said Baloo, although he was hurt. "Tell Bagheera the Master Words. First for the birds."

"*We are of one blood, you and I,*" Mowgli whistled and chirped.

"Very good!" said Baloo. "Now for the Snake-People."

"*We are of one blood,*" Mowgli answered with a great hissing. Then he jumped on Bagheera's back and made faces at Baloo.

"One of these days," Mowgli exclaimed, "I will have my own tribe, and we will throw branches and dirt at you, Baloo."

"*Whoof!*" Baloo's big paw scooped Mowgli from Bagheera's shoulders. "Mowgli, have you been talking with the Monkey-People? Answer me honestly!"

"One day, after you scolded me, the gray apes came down from the trees and said they wanted to be my friends," Mowgli sniffed.

Baloo's voice rumbled. "Man-cub, I have taught you the laws of all the Jungle-People, except for the Monkey-People. This is because they have no law. They are foolish boasters, and they are forbidden."

Far up in the trees, a group of monkeys chattered. One told the others how he had seen Mowgli weave sticks into a shelter. This was something the Monkey-People did not know how to do. Then one of them had an idea: if they captured Mowgli, they could make him their teacher.

When it was time for a nap, Mowgli lay down between his friends and fell asleep. The next thing he knew, he felt hands on his legs and arms—strong, hairy hands. Then he was staring down through swaying branches. The monkeys howled with triumph as they swung away with Mowgli.

The flight of the Monkey-People was incredible. The monkeys swung recklessly from tree to tree, up to a hundred feet above the ground. Two of them held Mowgli under his arms as they went. Mowgli was both sick and giddy from their speed. From the tops of the trees, he could see for miles across the Jungle.

As exciting as this was, Mowgli became angry. More than once, he thought the monkeys would drop him. Looking up and away, Mowgli saw Chil the Kite soaring nearby. Mowgli whistled, and Chil dropped down to investigate.

"*We are of one blood, you and I!*" Mowgli called, using the Master Words for the birds.

"Who are you, friend?" whistled Chil.

"I am Mowgli. Tell Baloo and Bagheera where I go!" Mowgli shrieked as the monkeys dipped back below the treetops. Chil rocked on his wings and watched.

Meanwhile, Bagheera and Baloo had lost sight of Mowgli.

"*Whoo!*" moaned Baloo. "Put dead bats on my head! I am miserable!" He clasped his head and rolled on the ground.

"You are acting like a porcupine!" scolded Bagheera. "Let us think of a plan."

"I *am* a fool!" said Baloo, sitting up. "The Monkey-People do not fear us, because we cannot move through the trees. But there is one who they *do* fear. Let us find Kaa."

Baloo and Bagheera soon found Kaa the Python stretched out on a warm ledge, looking shiny and splendid with the thirty feet of his body twisted into great muscular loops.

Baloo stepped up to Kaa and sat down. "Good hunting!" cried Baloo.

"Good hunting to us all," the snake answered sleepily. "Is there game afoot?"

"We are hunting," Baloo said casually.

"Then allow me to come with you. I am so big now that a branch snapped during my last hunt. My tail was not wrapped

around the tree, and the noise
of my falling woke the Monkey-People.
They called me evil names."

"Yes. Like . . . footless, yellow earthworm," said Bagheera under
his whiskers, as though he were trying to remember something.

"Sssssss! They call me *that?*" demanded Kaa.

"Oh, yes," said Bagheera.

Then Bagheera cut to the point: "The trouble is this, Kaa.
Those pickers of palm leaves have stolen away our man-cub."

"He is the best and boldest, and my own pupil," said Baloo.
"We love him, Kaa."

"I too know what love is," said Kaa. "These monkeys are
foolish, and careless. We must remind them who their
masters are."

"Look up!" cried a voice above them. The three looked up, and
saw Chil swooping overhead.

"I have seen a man-cub," whistled Chil. "He asked me to find you.
The monkeys have taken him to the Cold Lairs." Few of the Jungle-
People went to the Cold Lairs. It was an ancient, deserted city,
buried deep in the Jungle.

"Thank you, Chil!" cried Baloo. The kite wheeled away into the
afternoon sun.

"We must go quickly," said Bagheera. With that, he set off into
the Jungle at a brisk canter. Kaa matched his speed, slithering
powerfully along the ground. Baloo soon fell behind.
Panting, he promised to catch up as soon as he could.

The monkeys dragged Mowgli into the Cold Lairs in the late afternoon. The monkeys called this their city, yet they did not know how the buildings were meant to be used. They would sit in the king's throne-room and scratch for fleas. Or they would explore, but would immediately forget where they had just been. The city's battlements were tumbled down, and vines hung from the windows of the now-roofless palace. But even in ruin, it was still splendid.

The monkeys put Mowgli on a white marble terrace. He could not help laughing as they began to tell him how wise they were. The monkeys gathered by the hundreds to listen to each other.

"We are great!" they shouted. "We are the most wonderful people of the Jungle! We all say so, so it must be true!" The monkeys shouted and danced all afternoon, swinging each other by the arms. Mowgli kept silent, sure that they were all crazy.

Daylight faded. As the monkeys lounged around him in circles fifty or sixty deep, jabbering, Mowgli wondered how the night would end.

Suddenly he heard Bagheera's light feet on the terrace. Without warning, the black panther began striking left and right at the monkeys with his powerful paws. There were howls of fright and rage. Then Bagheera tripped on the wriggling bodies beneath him.

"There is only one! Attack him!" screamed the monkeys.

Biting and pulling, a mass of monkeys closed over Bagheera. Mowgli thrashed as six monkeys pulled him away. They tossed him into a ruined summerhouse, through a hole in the domed roof, where the entrance was blocked and he could not climb out.

Then from another wall rose a bear's roar. Old Baloo had arrived! He jumped on a trio of monkeys and gave them a big bear-hug. With a *whoosh*, the air rushed from their lungs and they collapsed. Baloo waded into the next wave, throwing monkeys this way and that.

But the monkeys kept coming. Soon the panther was trapped in a corner, and the bear was covered by furious Monkey-People. Mowgli's heart beat in his throat.

Then, out of nowhere, came Kaa. A python can strike a blow with his head, like a battering-ram. A python four or five feet long can knock a man down. Kaa was thirty feet long, a half-ton of pure muscle. Kaa delivered his first blow to the crowd around Baloo. Monkeys flew everywhere.

The monkeys had feared Kaa for generations, so they scattered, chattering with terror. Baloo sighed with relief, and helped Mowgli from his prison.

But Kaa was not done. He opened his mouth and spoke one long, hissing word. Up in the trees, on the walls, and on the broken buildings, the monkeys froze where they were. It was eerily silent in the Cold Lairs. The python turned to look at Mowgli.

"Mowgli, this is Kaa, to whom we owe our lives," said Bagheera.

"*We are of one blood, you and I,*" said Mowgli respectfully. "If you are ever hungry, I will hunt for you, O great Kaa. I will repay the debt I owe to you."

"Thanks, Little Brother," said Kaa, his eyes twinkling. "You have a brave heart and a courteous tongue. Now it grows late. But before we go, I must attend to one last piece of business."

Kaa glided to the center of the terrace. He snapped his jaws.

"Now, Monkey-People, begins the Dance of Kaa. You will not forget that Kaa is your master!"

Humming one note, the python turned in a big circle, weaving his head from left to right. Then he began making loops and figure eights. Then came soft, oozy triangles that melted into squares and other fantastic shapes. Kaa never stopped moving, never stopped his hum. Mowgli watched in wonder.

"Monkey-People, can you move?" asked the voice of Kaa.

The monkeys were frozen, their eyes glazed. "No, O Kaa!" they whispered in unison.

"Good!" said Kaa. "Come one pace toward me."

Hypnotized, all the monkeys took one step forward. Baloo and Bagheera felt Kaa's magic, too, and swayed on their feet. Mowgli put his hands on their shoulders, to wake them. Together, the three of them turned away. As they left the Cold Lairs, they heard Kaa command the monkeys never to bother the man-cub again.

When they were some distance away, they sat down. Mowgli saw that Baloo and Bagheera were tired and sore.

"I was bad to mock you, and disobey your wishes," said Mowgli sorrowfully.

"Yes, you have been bad. Feel sorrowful, for that is the Law," said Bagheera. Mowgli felt terrible, and stared at the ground.

After a few moments, Baloo said: "There. That is enough. We are satisfied, Mowgli. Now give me a smile." Mowgli slowly raised his head, and saw his teacher beaming with love.

"Come," said Bagheera, "jump on my back, Little Brother, and we will go home."

Mowgli did, and laid his head down on Bagheera's shoulder. He drifted off and slept deeply, even when his friends put him down in his own cave.

How Fear Came

The Law of the Jungle is the oldest law in the world. One year, Mowgli saw for himself how important the Law really is.

It began when the spring rains failed to come. Inch by inch, a cruel heat crept into the Jungle. The plants turned yellow and then brown. Chil brought desperate news: the sun was killing the Jungle in every direction.

By the summer, the Waingunga River had dwindled to a trickle. Hathi the Elephant stood watch on the bank, waiting. One morning he saw what he was looking for. It was a ridge of blue rock poking from the center of the river—the Peace Rock, exposed in the low water.

Then Hathi lifted his trunk and proclaimed the Water Truce. By the Law, the river was a safe refuge during the Water Truce. No animal could hunt there, for every animal needs water.

All the Jungle-People drank from the still, dirty water, and then sat on the banks, too tired to move. On one side of the river were the deer, buffalo, pigs, porcupines, and others who ate green things. The other bank was for the hunters—the wolves, snakes, hawks, and big cats. Mowgli and Bagheera sat down near them. In the center of the river stood Hathi and his three sons, gray in the moonlight.

"Hathi, have you ever seen a drought like this?" asked Baloo wearily.

"It will pass," said Hathi.

"There is little for the man-cub to eat," Baloo said, motioning to Mowgli.

"Good!" said a voice. It was Shere Khan, coming down to the river for a drink. He watched with pleasure as his arrival sent a shiver of nervousness through the deer on the opposite bank.

"Bah!" spat Bagheera. "What trouble do you bring?"

"Tonight I hunt humans," said Shere Khan coolly. "On this night, it is my right."

Hathi narrowed his little eyes. "I know. But the river is to drink, not to boast. Begone!" The tiger slowly sauntered away.

As courteously as he could, Mowgli asked: "Hathi, what does Shere Khan mean? To hunt humans is always shameful."

Hathi stood still in the river bed, tall and wrinkled. "Of all things, we fear humans the most," he said. All the animals murmured in agreement.

"This matter has to do with you," whispered Bagheera to Mowgli.

"It does not! I'm not a human. I'm a member of the Wolf-Pack!" said Mowgli.

"And why do we fear humans?" Hathi went on. "I will tell you the tale. In the beginning of the world, the only animal was Tha, the First Elephant. There was mud all around, but Tha pulled trees out of the mud and made the Jungle.

"Then the other animals came. In those first days, all the animals walked together. No animal feared another. Everyone ate fruit and flowers. Everything was peaceful.

Hathi looked into the starlit sky. "Tigers are jealous of humans all year, and so they hunt humans when they can. Tonight is the night when tigers are not afraid of humans," he said. Then Hathi dipped his trunk into the water as a sign that he did not wish to talk any more.

Mowgli jumped onto Baloo's back. "Why have you never told me this story?" he demanded.

"Because the Jungle is full of such tales. There is no end to them. Now let go of my ear."

"Tiger! Tiger!"

The drought passed, and so did the years, until Mowgli was eleven years old. Mowgli was young and strong, and took his place at the Council Rock. But sometimes his friends worried for his safety.

"Shere Khan has been making friends with the younger wolves. He flatters them and gives them food," said Bagheera one afternoon. "Akela would stop this if he could, but he has grown old. Today, in front of the Pack, he failed to make a kill, a sign of weakness.

"The Pack must have a new leader soon. That tiger will try to turn the Pack against you and Akela. I have heard the rumors."

"Why would anyone in the Pack turn against me?" questioned Mowgli. "I obey the Law. I have helped all the wolves!"

"Remember Hathi's story," said Bagheera. "The others hate you because you are a human. They know that humans know things and can do things that animals cannot. Feel under my chin."

Under Bagheera's silky fur, Mowgli felt a little bald spot.

"No one in the Jungle knows I have that spot, except for you," Bagheera said. "It is the mark made by my collar.

"You see, I was born among humans, and was kept in a cage at the King's palace. I had never seen the Jungle. I watched the humans, and learned their ways. Then one night I realized that I was Bagheera, the Panther. I knew who I was. So I broke the lock, and came here to the Jungle, to my rightful home."

Mowgli's eyes were wide with wonder, and with confusion.

Bagheera looked at Mowgli tenderly. "Man-cub, some day you will have to live with humans. You will find your place. But first you must worry about Shere Khan. I know something that will help. You must get the Red Flower."

By this Bagheera meant fire. No creature in the Jungle will call fire by its proper name. Every beast is terrified of it, and invents other ways of describing it.

"The Red Flower?" said Mowgli. "I know what it is. It grows outside the huts of the villagers, in little pots."

"You are clever!" Bagheera said proudly. "Yes, get some quickly, and keep it until you need it."

Mowgli ran through the forest until he came to the edge of the village. He scuttled up to the window of the nearest hut, and plucked out an earthen pot filled with glowing coals. Before long he was back at his cave.

All day, Mowgli faithfully fed the fire with twigs. He also found a strong, dry branch. After the sun set, Mowgli heard many wolf-howls. He picked up his branch and pot and went to the Council Rock.

There he saw Akela, weak and tired, lying beside his rock. This meant that leadership of the Pack was open. Shere Khan and his many new wolf-friends strutted to and fro. To the side, Mowgli saw Father and Mother Wolf and his brothers. He could tell that they did not like what they saw. Bagheera sat by silently.

Shere Khan began to speak, but Mowgli cut him off.

"Free People," he cried, "does Shere Khan lead the Pack? What has a tiger to do with our affairs?"

"What does a man-cub have to do with our affairs?" replied Shere Khan angrily. His wolf-allies howled with approval.

Akela lifted his head. "He has eaten and slept as a wolf. He has kept the Law."

"No human cub can run with the Jungle-People!" howled Shere Khan. "Give him to me!"

"He is a human! A human!" snarled many of the wolves. They began to gather behind Shere Khan. Bagheera, Mother and Father Wolf, and their friends were outnumbered.

"Fighting will come soon," whispered Father Wolf to Mowgli. "It is up to you."

Mowgli stood tall, the fire-pot in his hands.

"Listen!" he cried to the Pack. "I have always lived as a wolf. But tonight you have told me that I am a human. So do not call me a member of the Pack any more! I am a human, and I can do the things that humans can do!"

Mowgli thrust the dead branch into the fire-pot. Immediately it caught fire and became a blazing torch. His long black hair tossing over his shoulders, his torch throwing off sparks, Mowgli was a fearsome sight. Shere Khan and the wolves drew back in terror.

Mowgli's eyes flashed with anger. "I will leave the Jungle, and live among my own kind. But hear this: there will be no fighting in the Pack. Before I go, here is a reminder."

Mowgli strode up to Shere Khan. The tiger was paralyzed with fright. Gritting his teeth with contempt, Mowgli thrust out his torch and singed the tiger's whiskers.

"Next time you will not be so lucky!" Mowgli vowed. Whirling the torch to the left and to the right, he chased away Shere Khan and the traitorous wolves. Soon only Akela, Bagheera, and the handful of faithful wolves were left.

Mowgli sat down. Something was hurting inside him. He began to sob.

"What is this?" he said. "I do not want to leave the Jungle. What is happening to me, Bagheera?"

The panther sat down next to him. He said gently: "These are tears, Mowgli. Humans use them. They are only tears; let them fall."

"I will go to the village." He hugged his parents tightly.

"I have always loved you," said Mother Wolf. "Come back soon!"

Mowgli nodded. "I will!"

Dawn was beginning to break. Standing straight and proud, Mowgli went down the hillside alone, to meet those mysterious animals called humans.

In the Village

Mowgli walked until he came to the farmlands. They sat on a plain, where cattle and buffalo grazed. At one end of a ravine stood the village, and at the other end was the edge of the Jungle.

Mowgli went to the village gate and sat down. Soon a priest walked by, a fat man dressed in white. Mowgli opened his mouth and pointed to it, to show that he was hungry. The priest's jaw dropped with surprise. A crowd soon gathered, and all the people stared, talking, and pointing at Mowgli.

"These people have no manners," thought Mowgli. "They act like the monkeys."

"How wild he looks," said the priest. One woman observed: "But look at his eyes. They are fierce, but intelligent. Messua, he reminds me of your boy, the one taken by the tiger."

Messua, a woman with copper bracelets on her wrists and ankles, peered at Mowgli. "It was long ago when we lost our son in the Jungle. It is hard to tell. Yet he looks very much like my boy."

The priest was a clever man, so he said, "What the Jungle has taken, the Jungle has restored. Take the boy into your home. And do not forget to reward the priest, who cares for his people."

Mowgli thought that Messua looked kind, and so he followed her home. Messua gave Mowgli some milk and a piece of bread. As Mowgli ate, she laid her hand on his head.

"Are you really my son, Nathoo?" she said. "Do you remember me?" Mowgli did not recognize the name she called him.

"Perhaps it does not matter. From now on, I will treat you as my son," she said with tears in her eyes.

"What good is it to be a man if I cannot understand man's talk?" Mowgli thought. "I must learn."

Over the next days, Mowgli learned quickly. As soon as Messua said a word, Mowgli repeated it, almost perfectly. "Baloo would be proud of me," Mowgli thought with some sadness.

Living with humans was strange. At first, Mowgli refused to sleep in the hut, because it seemed too much like a cage or a trap. Messua's husband, a trader, understood.

"Nathoo has never seen a bed, Messua. Let him do as he wishes for now. With time, he will understand." So Mowgli slept behind the hut, under the stars.

For three months, Mowgli studied the ways of the village. He wore clothes, which he did not like, and he learned to plow. The children of the village made fun of him because he was different, but Mowgli ignored them. He remembered the Law of the Jungle, which says that it is never fair to take revenge on those who are weaker. And among the villagers, Mowgli was as strong as a bull.

Every evening a group of people gathered under a big fig tree. They told stories, especially Buldeo, the village's chief hunter. With his rifle next to him, Buldeo told fantastic, outrageous stories about animals, and what he had seen them do. The eyes of the children bulged with wonder. Mowgli, who knew how the animals really lived, had to stifle his laughter with both his hands.

"Oho! It is the jungle brat!" said Buldeo.

"If you are so wise, bring me the hide of the tiger who kills our cattle. Better yet, brat, don't talk when your elders speak." Mowgli recognized a braggart when he saw one.

As time passed, Mowgli began to feel very comfortable. Messua and her husband told Mowgli stories about the world beyond the Jungle, where there were oceans, and great iron beasts called trains. Sitting near the hearth, they were a warm presence in a way that Mother and Father Wolf, despite their great love, had never been.

Soon Mowgli was ready to go to work. So, early each morning, Mowgli rode on the back of Rama, the great herd bull, and led the cattle and buffalo out of the village. He drove them to the Waingunga River, where the buffalo wallowed in the mud.

One morning he saw a wolf waiting near the river. It was Gray Brother, the oldest of Mother and Father Wolf's cubs.

"I have been waiting to see you," said Gray Brother. "I bring bad news. Last night Shere Khan bragged to a jackal that he will ambush you tonight near the entrance to the village. Right now Shere Khan is sleeping in the ravine."

"Has he eaten?" asked Mowgli.

"Yes."

"Then he will be slow," said Mowgli. "This is my chance to put an end to him."

"I have brought a wise friend," said Gray Brother. A familiar face stepped from the brush.

"Akela!" said Mowgli, clapping his hands. "It is good to see you. I have a plan, and I need your help. Cut the herd in two, so the bulls are by themselves."

The two wolves ran in and out of the herd, barking and howling. Soon they had herded the cows and calves into one group, and the bulls into another.

Mowgli slipped onto Rama's back. "Gray Bother! Drive the cows into the ravine, to a place where the sides are higher than Shere Khan can jump. Then keep them there."

"Shall we take the bulls around?" panted Akela.

"Yes!" Mowgli yelled. And with that, he and Akela drove the thundering herd of cattle and buffalo into the forest. Mowgli's plan was simple. He and Akela would circle the bulls around to the far end of the ravine. With them at one end, and Gray Brother's herd of cows blocking the other end, Shere Khan would be trapped.

They soon came to the far end of the ravine. Mowgli called into the ravine. After a long time came a sleepy snarl.

"Who calls?" said Shere Khan.

From Rama's back he cried: "I, Mowgli! It is time for you to answer for all the trouble you have caused!"

Mowgli turned to Akela. "*Go!*" he shouted.

Akela gave his best howl, and the bulls thundered down into the ravine. Their horns pointed ahead, they filled the ravine from side to side. Mowgli whooped and urged them on. Once started, there was no stopping the herd.

Shere Khan heard the thunder of hooves. He lumbered down the ravine looking for an escape, but the walls were too high, and there was no way out. Turning in rage, Shere Khan saw Mowgli riding down on him. The tiger snarled, and then the herd of bulls flowed over him like a wave.

The herd stampeded on, and slowed only when it reached the herd of cows at the other end of the ravine. There Mowgli dismounted. With Gray Brother and Akela, he walked back to Shere Khan's body. The tiger was dead.

Mowgli sat down next to the body and unsheathed his knife. "I must take his hide to the Council Rock."

There was a noise around the corner of the ravine, and the two wolves hid themselves. Mowgli soon saw Buldeo.

"You let the herd stampede!" the hunter yelled at Mowgli. "You are worthless!"

But when he saw Shere Khan's body, Buldeo's face lit up. "There is a reward of a hundred rupees for his hide!" he said. "Well, I will overlook your stupidity. Perhaps I will give you one rupee if you carry the tiger's hide back for me."

"I need the hide for my own use," said Mowgli.

"That is no way to talk to the village hunter, boy!" roared Buldeo. "You need a beating!" He reached for Mowgli.

"This man is bothering me, Akela," was all Mowgli said.

Buldeo found himself on his back, looking up into the face of a very angry wolf.

"A wolf who obeys a boy! It is sorcery!" thought Buldeo. He lay as still as he could, expecting that Mowgli would turn into an animal, too.

"Great King!" the hunter said. "Forgive me! I did not know! Will your servant eat me?"

"No," said Mowgli, bending over the tiger's body. "Go in peace."

Buldeo hurried to the village, looking back over his shoulder the whole way. When he got there, he told a tale of magic and sorcery that made the priest look very grave.

It was nearly evening when Mowgli was done. He and the wolves drove the herd back toward the village. But at the village gate, they were greeted with a shower of stones.

The villagers shouted: "Sorceror! Jungle demon! Go away!"

Buldeo's rifle went off, and Mowgli could hear the bullet whiz overhead.

"Last time it was because I was a human. Now it is because I am a wolf!" said Mowgli. "Akela, Gray Brother, let us go."

"Do not leave, my son!" Mowgli could hear Messua's voice rise above the crowd's cries.

"Farewell!" called Mowgli. And he and the wolves trotted away into the Jungle.

The moon was going down when they reached the Council Rock. There they saw Mother and Father Wolf.

"They have cast me out from their Man-pack," shouted Mowgli. "But I have defeated Shere Khan."

"I am glad you have returned," said Mother Wolf.

"Little Brother, you have done well!" said a silky voice. Bagheera came running to Mowgli.

"Look well, O Wolves!" Akela cried into the Jungle. Slowly, the wolves came to the Council Rock. Some limped from being caught in traps. Others were mangy from eating bad food. The Pack had been without leadership, and had fallen on hard times. There at the Council Rock, they saw Mowgli and Akela sitting on Shere Khan's hide.

"We are tired of lawlessness," they said. "Be our wise guide, Akela. And lead us, too, Man-cub."

"I do not think I can lead you," said Mowgli. "But I will make the Jungle my home again." At the edge of the Council, Bagheera purred with satisfaction.

Letting in the Jungle

The next day, Mowgli sat at the cave of Mother and Father Wolf. He told of his adventures in the village, as his friends listened with delight.

That afternoon, Akela trotted up. "Chil has brought news," he said. "The men in the village are buzzing like hornets. They all carry guns, and the Red Flower has blossomed at the village gate."

"Why? They have already cast me out," said Mowgli angrily.

"They are blinded by fear," said Akela. "They will hunt you, and us. We are all in danger."

"I must see for myself," said Mowgli.

At dusk, he slipped to the edge of the village. He could see two guards standing watch outside Messua's door. Why were they there? Creeping closer, Mowgli heard them talking about Messua.

"That boy was a sorcerer," said the first. "The animals obeyed him."

The second guard agreed. "The woman must be a witch. She took care of the boy, and she must have known all along. The trial will be an easy one. She will be found guilty."

Silently, Mowgli slipped to the hut's back window. It was tied shut from the outside, so he cut the rope.

Messua and her husband saw him. "Make no noise," Mowgli whispered. "If you get out of here, is there a place you can go?"

"Yes," said Messua's husband. "I have friends in Kanhiwara, a town thirty miles from here. We will be safe there. But what about all the people here? Superstition has made them crazy."

"Wait here until I return," said Mowgli. And he slipped away as silently as he had come. His face burning with anger, he ran straight to the river. Soon he found Hathi and his three sons.

"Good hunting," said Hathi, in his dignified way.

"Hathi, when I was in the village, I heard a story. Years ago, a great elephant fell into a trap. A sharpened stake in the pit cut him, from his heel all the way to his shoulder. Men took him away, and made him a slave. But the elephant broke his ropes and escaped."

Mowgli put his hand on Hathi's great side. Running down it was a long, white scar.

"It was you, wasn't it, Hathi?"

"Why have you come to me, Mowgli?"

Mowgli's face was grim. "You know how cruel humans can be. They have turned against the woman who took me in. And they will soon come with the Red Flower, burn the trees, and hunt the Jungle-People. I will not allow it."

Hathi stood silent for a time. Then he said: "The villagers have always used the Jungle according to their whims. Each year they grow bolder. But the Jungle is our home. They must not be allowed to endanger it. We must let in the Jungle."

Hathi raised his trunk and trumpeted his war cry. The call spread across the Jungle.

At dawn, Mowgli stood at the edge of the Jungle and surveyed the village.

"Is everyone ready?" he asked. Baloo nodded. As Baloo waited, Mowgli and Mother Wolf slipped to the edge of the village and hid. Suddenly, a babble of confused voices arose on the other side of the village. The guards at Messua's hut went to investigate.

Mowgli ran to the back of Messua's hut. He helped Messua and her husband through the window and took them toward the Jungle. There, Mother Wolf leaped from her hiding place.

Messua gasped, but Mowgli took her hand. "This is also my mother," he said. "She wishes to repay your kindness to me. Follow her, and you will be safe." Messua kissed Mowgli on the cheek. Then she and her husband followed Mother Wolf into the Jungle.

Soon Mowgli could hear the villagers shouting: "The fields! The fields! Come quickly!"

The villagers had good reason to be alarmed. An army of wild pigs and deer had swept out of the Jungle, and were merrily eating everything in the fields.

A mob assembled. "This is the work of the witch-woman!" someone yelled. "She has turned the Jungle against us!" The crowd rushed up the street, waving clubs and knives. Buldeo led the mob.

The crowd tore open the door to Messua's hut. But she was not there. Instead, stretched out full length on the bed, was an enormous black panther. The crowd stared in desperate silence. Bagheera looked up slowly, his eyes glinting. He yawned grandly, showing his gleaming, sharp fangs. The next second the crowd was gone, and Bagheera had leaped back through the window while the panicked crowd scattered.

Then Hathi and his sons crashed through the village gate. Behind them was a great herd of hundreds of porcupines, bats, water buffalo, cobras, birds, bears, monkeys, and wolves, led by Kaa.

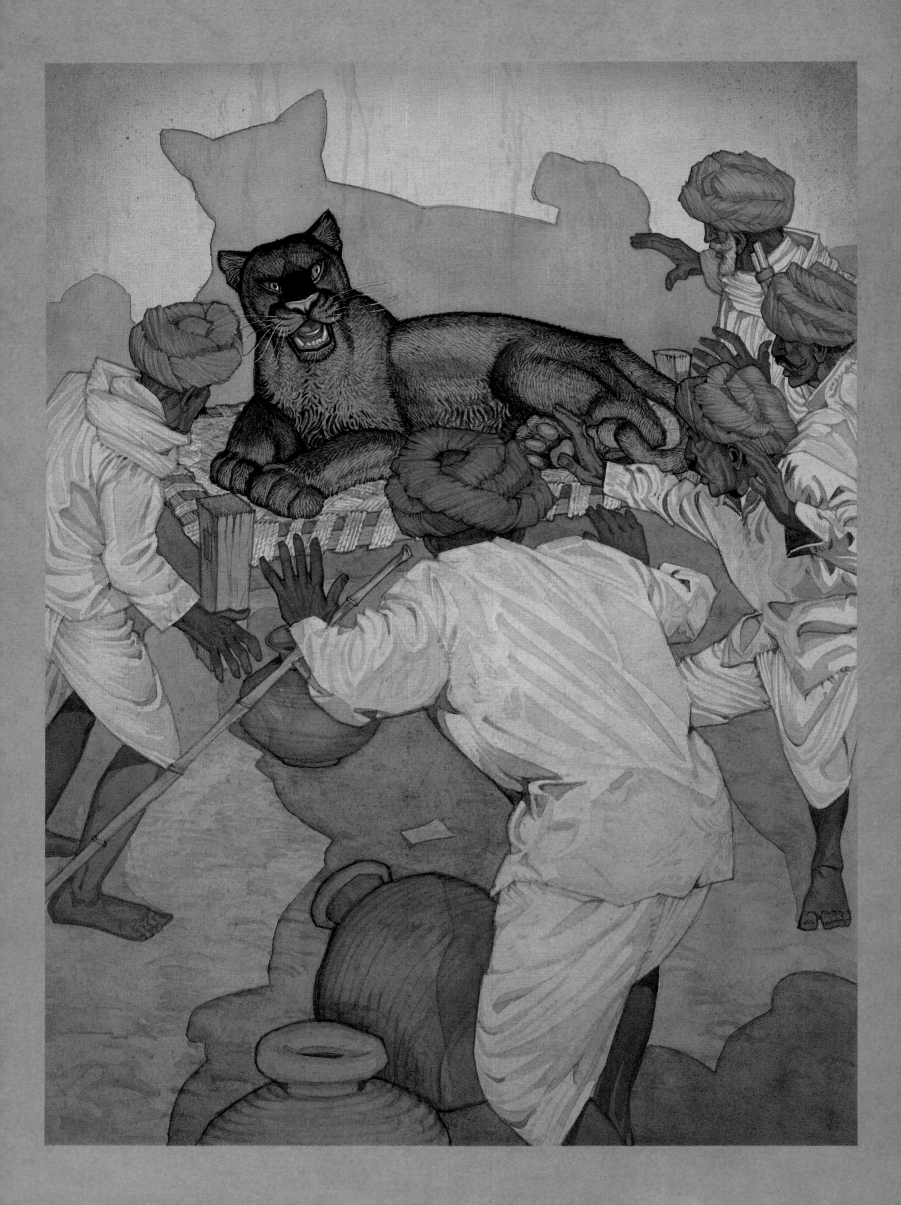

The animals chased the terrified villagers in and out of the huts and through the town, hooting and howling and nipping at their heels. When they reached the far side of the village, the animals returned to the Jungle.

When the dust cleared, the stunned villagers looked around them. The village had been turned inside-out, and the crops had been eaten. Not one shoot remained in the fields.

"We took from the Jungle, and now the Jungle has taken back," said the priest. "There are no more crops. We must settle elsewhere." The villagers began to pack their belongings. From the forest they could hear, but could not understand, cries of celebration from the Jungle-People.

The Spring Running

In the Indian jungle, the seasons slide one into the other almost without division. And so the autumn turned to winter, and winter turned to spring. Akela died of old age, and the Pack elected a new leader.

Early one spring morning, Mowgli and Bagheera sat far up on a hill overlooking the river. The morning mists lay below them in bands of white and green.

"Spring returns at last," said Bagheera. The panther rolled onto his back and beat the air with his paws.

"You're acting like a kitten," teased Mowgli.

"And you?" said Bagheera. "Doesn't the spring make you happy?"

Mowgli did not respond. He sat with his head in his hands, looking out over the valley.

Bagheera crouched next to Mowgli. "There is no fire in your eyes," said the panther. "You look distant, and do not run with me."

Mowgli continued to stare across the Jungle. "I have been thinking about my place," he said. "I will visit the town that Messua fled to. I will see how far the Man-pack has changed."

Bagheera rested his head in Mowgli's lap for a moment. Then without a sound, he got up and bounded away into the Jungle, to let Mowgli go his own way.

Mowgli peered at the town of Kanhiwara from a field of tall crops. A girl about his age, dressed in white, came down a path. As she passed, she caught sight of Mowgli. Startled, she screamed with surprise because she thought she had seen a spirit. Mowgli backed noiselessly into the high crops and watched her, fascinated, until she was out of sight.

In the village, after some searching, Mowgli found Messua's hut. He cried softly, "Messua! O Messua!"

"Nathoo?" said a quivering voice. The door flew open, and there was the woman who had been so good to Mowgli.

She took Mowgli's hand and led him inside. "We owe our lives to you," she said. "The wolf led us through the Jungle, safe and sound, and we have a new life here. But we have missed you."

"I have missed you, too," said Mowgli. "I want to come back. But first I must say goodbye to my friends."

Atop the Council Rock, Mowgli's face was streaked with tears of happiness, and tears of pain.

"Your trail ends here, Manling?" said Kaa.

Mowgli leaned his head against Kaa's great coils. "I have learned that there are good people and bad in the human world, just as there are good and bad Jungle-People," said Mowgli.

"I look in the water of the river and see my reflection. And when I do, I know that I must live among humans." Mowgli wiped at the tears on his cheeks.

"There is wisdom in your words," said Kaa. "But know that wherever you go, we are of one blood, you and I."

"Thank you, my brother," said Mowgli.

"Mowgli," said old Baloo, "my eyes do not see well these days, but in my mind I can see far. I see you making your own trail, among your own kind, as a just and kind leader. But if ever you need a wing to carry a message, or a friendly paw—remember that the Jungle-People are here to help."

Mowgli looked from face to face in the circle gathered around him—at Gray Brother, at Mother Wolf and Father Wolf, at Chil, and at Kaa and Baloo. They were such friends as no other human had ever known.

Just at that moment, there was a crash in the thicket. Light and strong as always, Bagheera appeared at their side. He purred and licked Mowgli's hand.

"Remember that Bagheera loves you," the panther cried, and bounded away. At the foot of the hill he cried again, loud and long, "Good hunting!"

Mowgli joyfully hugged Baloo. "I will never forget any of you. I promise!"

"Let us go with you to the edge of the Jungle," said Gray Brother. "Today we all follow new trails."

The End

© 1994 by Running Press
Illustrations © 1994 by Don Daily

All rights reserved under the Pan-American and
International Copyright Conventions

Printed in China

*This book may not be reproduced in whole or in part, in any form or
by any means, electronic or mechanical, including photocopying, recording,
or by any information storage and retrieval system now known or
hereafter invented, without written permission from the publisher.*

9 8 7 6 5 4 3 2
Digit on the right indicates the number of this printing

Library of Congress Cataloging-in-Publication Number
93-087601

ISBN 0-7624-1495-2

Cover design by Frances J. Soo Ping Chow
Interior design by Nancy Loggins Gonzalez
Typography: Bembo with Mona Lisa Recut
        by Deborah Lugar

This book may be ordered by mail from the publisher.
But try your bookstore first!

Published by Courage Books, an imprint of
Running Press Book Publishers
125 South Twenty-second Street
Philadelphia, Pennsylvania 19103-4399

Visit us on the web!
www.runningpress.com